Crush

Carrie Mac

orca soundings

ORCA BOOK PUBLISHERS

Library and Archives Canada Cataloguing in Publication

Mac, Carrie, 1975-

Crush / Carrie Mac.

(Orca soundings)
ISBN 10: 1-55143-521-7 (bound).--ISBN 13: 978-1-55143-521-3 (bound)
ISBN 10: 1-55143-526-8 (pbk.).--ISBN 13: 978-1-55143-526-8 (pbk.)

I. Title. II. Series.
PS8625.A23C78 2006   jC813'.6   C2006-900405-6

First published in the United States, 2006
Library of Congress Control Number: 2006921005

Summary: During a summer in New York, Hope falls in love
with another girl and must decide whether she is gay.

Orca Book Publishers gratefully acknowledges the support for its
publishing programs provided by the following agencies: the Government
of Canada through the Book Publishing Industry Development Program
and the Canada Council for the Arts, and the Province of British Columbia
through the BC Arts Council and the Book Publishing Tax Credit.

Cover design by Lynn O'Rourke
Cover photography by Getty Images

ORCA BOOK PUBLISHERS
PO BOX 5626, STN.B
VICTORIA, BC CANADA
V8R 6S4

ORCA BOOK PUBLISHERS
PO BOX 468
CUSTER, WA USA
98240-0468

www.orcabook.com
Printed and bound in Canada.
Printed on 100% PCW recycled paper.
11 10 09 08 • 6 5 4 3

For Brooklyn

Chapter One

I have two suitcases, one backpack and a barking West Highland terrier in one of those dog-carrying bags movie stars made cool. Daisy started barking when she got into the car, and she hasn't stopped since. What if she barks all the way to New York? That will make me popular on the flight.

"Have you got everything?" Mom rifles through her backpack. "I thought I had gum in here for you."

"I have gum, Mom."

"Chew this on the way up and down." She hands me a pack of sugar-free bubble gum. "It'll help with your ears."

"I know, Mom. Thanks." Their luggage is stacked in a teetering pile and looks like it's about to collapse. "How much time do you have?"

"An hour or so before check-in." She checks and rechecks their passports. Daisy barks and barks.

They're going to Thailand to build a school. I'm going to New York to stay with my sister for the summer. Of course, I wish I was going to Thailand, but it's my parents' thirtieth non-wedding (they're common-law) anniversary and that's what they chose to do for it. I was not invited. When they announced their plans, I just assumed I'd be going along with them, and they just assumed that I wouldn't be. For three months I thought I was going to spend the summer in Thailand, only to find out a month ago that I was going to spend the summer in Brooklyn, with my spacey older sister and her failed-actor boy-friend. What fun.

"How are you feeling, sweetheart?" Dad puts an arm across my shoulder. He's the one who finally realized the misunderstanding and filled me in. I wasn't impressed, to say the least. "Doing okay, kiddo?"

And Daisy barks and barks and barks.

"I'm fine, Dad."

"I know you're upset about this." He squats to peer at Daisy in her little carrying case. "Blessed creature, be quiet!" He stands again. Daisy barks and barks and barks. "But I also know that you understand how important it is for your mother and me to share this experience together, as a couple."

My dad, professional therapist.

"I know, Dad."

"Some things in life are best experienced solely with your life partner, to strengthen intimacy and create shared memories upon which to build a deeper love," he says.

I roll my eyes. What else do you do when you're seventeen and your father says something like that?

"Yeah, Dad. Got it."

"I know you do, sweetheart." He kisses my forehead. "You are my brilliant star."

Mom is back from the very expensive airport store with more goodies for my flight.

"Tissues, trashy magazines, mini sewing kit—you never know—crossword puzzle book, hard candies. I couldn't find any sugar- free. Be sure to brush extra hard."

I stuff them into my backpack, which is already bursting with all of the goodies she'd packed for me at home.

"And an umbrella." She hands me a super- compact little thing, hot pink. "We forgot to pack one."

"Joy will have umbrellas," I say.

"Your sister…" Dad says.

"Your sister…" Mom says.

"And that Bruce…" Dad says.

"Bruce, Bruce, Bruce." Mom shakes her head.

"Okay, okay. I'll try to fit it in." I jam it into my pack. Anything to get them off the subject of the not-so-happy couple.

"Sorry about the color," Mom says.

"Doesn't matter." I'll never open that umbrella over my head, but I love my mother enough to not say so. "Thanks."

Dad checks his watch. It's his first watch, ever. He bought it especially for their trip, and it has a GPS and all kinds of high-tech gadgets on it. Now, I love him to neurons, but my "Mr. Tie-Dye T-Shirt, Hemp Shorts and Sandals dad" is the last human on earth who should be allowed near anything high-tech or remotely electronic.

They're taking a satellite phone too, and a laptop, and I can only hope that my mother will not let him near any of it. Every once in a while, he decides he's going to become a technical genius—like now, for example.

Apparently he's forgotten about his latest spectacle, which involved $14,000 worth of solar panels dominoing off the roof and smashing to bits on the patio below. Of course, everyone was mad at him; it took forever to save up the money for the panels. But instead of bad vibes from everybody, he got sympathy because he slipped off the roof along with the solar panels and busted his leg in three places.

My mother unravels her orange sarong practically down to her underwear (thank the Universe, she's actually wearing some for once) and rearranges it. She's paired the sarong with a bright blue tank top that advertises her belly rolls like they're the aisle four special. Her skin is dark and leathery from years of sunshine working in the market garden, and she's wearing her usual assortment of wacky bangles and necklaces. My parents. I love them. But they look like lost, aging Dead Heads.

They're whispering to each other, holding hands, leaning in close, bodies touching. To look at them, you'd think they were falling in love before your very eyes. They kiss, and then my dad kisses his fingertip and touches it to her lips. He always does that, and it always makes me smile.

"Sweetheart?" Dad takes my hand. I feel a Circle coming on. "We love you so very, very much." He closes his eyes. "Let's do Circle." My mom closes her eyes too and lets out the same melodic sigh she does before every Circle.

We're not a religious family, per se, but we very much believe in the Universe, with a capital U. When I was little, Circle was one of my favorite things, and I didn't care where we did it—in the parking lot of the grocery store or in a theater lobby, what did I care? But now, the public ones are getting a little unbearable. I don't close my eyes. Instead, as my dad launches into his blessing, I soak in the gawks and stares here in International Departures. "Universe, we thank you for our precious Hope and ask that you keep her safe and healthy and happy during our time apart," Dad says. He lets out a little mumbly sound, which he always does, kind of like "Amen" for hippies.

"And take care of her while we're so far away," my mom says, taking her turn. "Because being apart will bruise all of our hearts."

Despite the audience, I get a little choked up when she says that. It suddenly occurs to me that we've never been separated for more than a week before. No sane teenager should be sad to get rid of her parents for a couple of months, but I am. Suddenly, this is the saddest event in modern times. "And, please, let Joy and Bruce find peace with each other and themselves." She always ends with that, no matter what the Circle is about.

Daisy barks and barks. It's my turn to say something, but if I open my mouth to speak, I'll just start crying. I close my eyes. Really, who cares who gawks? These are my parents—my best friends, really—who I love more than anyone else, and they're about to go to Thailand for two months all by themselves without me. What if there's another killer tsunami? What if they die from some tropical flesh-eating infection? What if they're mugged or drugged or imprisoned? What if Dad gets drunk and does something stupid and ends up stuck in some third world jail for the rest of his life? Or what if they just disappear without a trace? What if this is the last time I ever see them?

"Sweetheart?" Dad squeezes my hand again.

"Give me a sec?" The tears well instantly.

"Um. I thank the Universe…uh, for my amazing, wonderful, loving—" I start bawling.

And Daisy barks and barks.

My parents squeeze my hands but don't break Circle to comfort me. We've been through this before. If we're in Circle—it doesn't matter if it's just us or any of the others who do Circle (yes, there's a whole whack of us cool people)—we just let the person *be* with their emotions. That's the whole point, after all…to just *be* with the Universe. If you're raised by hippies, this sort of thing passes for normal.

I take a deep breath and launch into it before another rush of tears start. All of a sudden, I really need my parents to know how much I love them.

"I am so thankful that my parents love each other so much, and that they love me and Joy with all of their hearts. I know how blessed I am to have them and how lucky I am compared to the screwed-up homes so many kids have. I am so proud of them for going to Thailand to build a school and for being together for thirty years and for who they are in the Universe, and I just want them to be safe. And I want Dad to watch what he does when he's been drinking."

Sometimes Dad gets a little touchy when I mention his drinking, but when I open my eyes, they're both gazing at me adoringly. This usually drives me mad, but right now it just makes me miss them already.

"Blessed be," they say in unison.

"Blessed be," I mumble, through more tears.

We hug each other, and then we all start crying with the earnestness of years of practice. I bet the passersby think we're heading to a funeral, the way we're carrying on. But we carry on like this for any number of occasions: new babies, weddings, breakups, the tsunami, the global AIDS crisis, crop failure, or Joy getting a full scholarship to the Brooklyn Academy of Dance after we all thought she'd be a cokehead underwear model for the rest of her life, and of course partings especially, like this one.

It's time for me to head to the plane. New York, here I come. With Daisy, who's started barking again. She barks all the way onto the plane, too. Yep, we're going to be about as popular as the woman in front of me with the twin babies who both have the rosy cheeks of teething and the drippy noses and runny eyes of a head cold. What fun.

Chapter Two

I just got back from a little wander to see how first class flies, but the snooty flight attendant wouldn't let me in. Miraculously, Daisy isn't barking, although the babies in front of me are still crying and have been ever since takeoff. Daisy's snout is tucked under her paws, and she's snoring like I've never heard before. I take another little stroll to the back of the plane (you don't want to sit too long or you'll get a blood clot and die). When I get back to my seat, I notice that the twins are sleeping too now. The mom glances up and smiles apologetically. She looks ten miles beyond tired.

"If you need a hand when they wake up, just let me know," I whisper.

"Really?" She puts a hand to her heart. "Do you really mean that?"

I nod. "Babysitter extraordinaire at your service." We shake hands. "My name's Hope."

"Maira. And thank you." She pumps my hand. "I've been getting the most evil looks. It's just that they're—"

"Teething and have colds."

"Yes!" She pumps my hand even harder. "How did you know?"

"I've babysat about a million kids."

One of the babies stretches his legs and opens his eyes a little. Maira finally lets go of my hand to put a finger to her lips, but just then the pilot comes over the speaker to tell us, louder and with more enthusiasm than necessary, that we're ahead of schedule by five minutes. Both babies wake up, and the one in green opens his mouth and lets out a spectacularly loud wail for such a little guy. I glance back at my seat. Thankfully, Daisy is sleeping through it.

"Oh dear." Maira picks him up. "Here we go."

"How about I take him for a little walk?" I offer as the other one sticks his fist in his mouth and screws his eyes shut in preparation for a screaming fit.

"You're an angel," she says as she hands me the first baby. "This is Felix. He has sneezing fits, so don't be alarmed if he goes off."

Felix and I pace the aisles—not into first class though, even with a cutie in my arms—and when he finally falls back to sleep, I trade him for the other one.

"Avery." Maira hands the wailer to me. "Normally the quiet one."

I pace with Avery for a while, singing softly to him, until he finally calms down too. Back at Baby Central, Felix is asleep, his head lolled to the side, sucking his bottom lip in like babies do. Avery reaches for his mother and gabbles at her.

"Hope, the miracle worker." Maira takes him. "That's the happiest he's been in days!" Avery kicks his legs gleefully as Maira covers him in kisses. "How can we thank her, Avery? What do you think, baby boy?" She bounces him and looks up at me. "Where are you headed?"

"To stay with my sister for the summer." I perch myself on an armrest. "My parents are madly in love with each other and have jetted off to Thailand to build a school to celebrate their thirtieth anniversary."

Maira goes quiet and her eyes well up. She's crying? Why? What did I say? "That's so sweet," she says as she fishes a tissue out of the diaper bag and dabs her eyes. "I don't think I've heard anything so sweet in a long, long time. It's so nice to hear about people who can make love last."

Maybe the tears are about her relationship with the babies' dad? But I can't ask a complete stranger that. My dad would, but he does that for a living. I don't.

"Uh, yeah. I guess." Great, now she's crying harder. "Sorry?"

"No, don't apologize." She fishes for a fresh tissue. "Your parents have the right idea. Maybe if we all celebrated love more, it wouldn't end up dead so often."

Wow, am I ever curious now. "You want me to leave you alone?" I wish my dad were here. He'd know how to deal with this.

"No, no, no." She pats the empty seat beside her. "Have a seat." She wipes her eyes one more time. "Now, tell me all about yourself. How'd you get to be such an amazing baby handler?"

"I live in a commune. There's lots of kids."

"A *commune*?" She stares at me. "Tell me, is that hard for you? What kind of commune? Not a religious one, I hope. I hear awful things about those, marrying the girls off so young, abuse of all kinds."

"Standard garden-variety hippie kind." I glance back to check on Daisy. Still snoring. "That's kind of our little joke, actually. We run a market garden."

"Organic, of course," Maria says bitterly. "Right?"

"It is." I summon my little evil-hormones-pesticide-cancer-GMO speech and prepare to launch it. "Are you anti-organic or something?"

"Not at all. I'm all for it." She pulls out a jar of baby food. "See?" Organic mashed peas and squash. "Oh no, I'm not the one with the attitude about it."

Oooo, I am dying to meet this guy. I glance at her left hand. White gold band. Still married, so far. Or at least still wearing her ring. Part of me wants to come right out and ask her how her marriage is going, but most of me just wants to change the subject.

"So where are you and the babies going?" I ask.

"Home, thank god." She settles Avery back into his seat. "But enough about me."

"That's hardly anything, but okay."

"Tell me about life in a commune," she says. "Are you homeschooled?"

"Sort of. We have our own school at Larchberry."

"That's the commune?"

I nod. "And the school is called the

Larchberry Experience. The kids decide the curriculum, select the instructors, basically run the place. Once we spent an entire year researching all things Egyptian."

"And your parents are building a Larchberry Experience in Thailand?"

"Yep."

"God, I would love to meet your parents." Good grief, she's crying again. Postpartum depression maybe? "They sound so wonderful. We should all be so blessed." She brings Avery's fingers to her lips and kisses them. "Really, we all should be so blessed."

She's full of questions, and when she finds out I'm going to be staying in Brooklyn, just ten blocks from her, she takes Joy's phone number in case she needs a sitter. As the plane starts its descent, she gives me a list of NYC must-do's, and I hand back Avery and his various yuppie baby toys.

"Thank you, Hope." She hugs me. "You saved me on this flight." She writes down her phone number. "If you need anything while you're in New York, you just call me, okay?"

"Do you want some help off with the babies?" I ask.

"Oh, would you?" She hugs me again. "Of course you would. Yes, please. Thank you."

It isn't until I'm pushing her double stroller down the airport corridor that I really begin to wonder about Daisy. She's slept for almost four hours and still hasn't stirred. As we wait for the baggage to arrive, I try to wake her up, but she just keeps snoring.

"Do you think she's okay?" I ask Maira.

Maira peeks at her. "Did you give her tranquilizers?"

"No, my parents don't believe in that kind of thing."

"Are you sure?" She lifts Daisy's paw and lets it drop. "Sure reminds me of my mother when she takes her 'special' pills."

"Maybe—" My heart leaps, suddenly terrified. "Do you think someone drugged her?"

"You know what?" Maira nods. "I think you might be right."

"Who would do that?" I pull Daisy out of

the bag and cradle her. She's limp. "I have to get her to a vet!"

"Bags first, Hope." Maira puts a hand on my shoulder. "She's breathing fine, her nose is wet. She'll be okay."

"I can't believe this is happening!"

"It's okay, calm down." Maria nods at the carousel. "The bags are coming. Collect your luggage, and then you can take care of Daisy."

With my luck, my bag will be the last off, or worse, it'll be lost. The first bags tumble down and, miracle of miracles, mine shows up soon after.

"Off you go," Maira says as she helps me pile it onto a cart. "Call me, okay? Let me know how you're doing. And Daisy."

"Okay, bye." I practically run with the cart and Daisy to where Joy is waiting for me. I run right past her and out into the night.

"Where's your car?" I holler behind me. "Someone drugged Daisy!"

"Oh my god," Joy says, deadpan. "I don't think so, kiddo."

"It's true! Where's the car?"

"First of all," Joy catches up to me and grabs my arm, "you're making a scene. Second, I doubt someone drugged your stupid dog. And third, I sold the car."

"You *what*?"

Joy holds up her hand, manicured nails and a chunky bracelet and a wrist so skinny it is nearly translucent. "I don't want to hear it. Dad never said I had to keep it for a certain length of time or anything."

"You have no idea how hard it was for him to save up for that," I say. "I cannot believe you sold the car. How can you be so ungrateful, Joy?"

Joy gives me one of her precisely constructed glares.

"Whatever, Joy. That's between you and Dad." I hold up a floppy, snoring, drooling Daisy. "Look at her! We have to get her to a vet."

Joy uses the same perfect manicure to leisurely hail a cab. As the driver stuffs my luggage into the trunk, Joy gracefully descends into the backseat. Every move she makes is like a carefully choreographed slice of her very own personal ballet in which she is the prima donna, of course. How can she be ten years older than me and still be so stuck on herself?

"Park Slope, please." Joy gives him her address.

"We need to go to an emergency vet, Joy."

"Relax, okay? She'll come out of it."

"We don't know that!"

"Fine." She flips open her cell to call Bruce. "But you're paying, kiddo."

It's dawn by the time we leave the vet, with a groggy but happy Daisy and a bill for hundreds of dollars. The vet, a grandfatherly man with a long beard and thick glasses, agrees to let me pay for some and work off the rest. There goes my entire savings along with a great big chunk of my summer, which looks like it will be spent walking gimpy dogs and cleaning litter boxes. Joy, of course, refuses to pay even one penny. I doubt she could, anyway. She spends all her money on eating out and clothes, and drugs too, if she's being honest. She might not be a full-time cokehead at the moment, but she still snorts it. I can just tell. My parents really have no idea. They think she's clean. That's a joke. Well, she is *clean*, very clean, as in neat freak bordering on obsessive-compulsive, but drug-free? Not likely. Not our Joy.

Chapter Three

Bruce, the failed-actor boyfriend, is waiting for us when we finally drag ourselves through the door. Daisy is now the widest awake of all of us, bouncing from couch to chair to floor to lap. Bruce is very hungover. He shuffles around like a zombie, trying to put breakfast together, but he burns the toast, the coffee is sludge thick and the eggs are snotty.

"Way to go, Bruce." Joy pushes her plate away, untouched. "This sucks."

Bruce snorts, slams a plate of toast onto the table and stalks off into the kitchen.

"You hear me?" Joy yells after him. "It's inedible! Nice going, Mister Chef Man!"

I cringe. They are so mean to each other. I just don't get how someone who was raised at Larchberry can have a mean bone in her body. And Dad is a couples' therapist! How can Joy be such a cruel mess?

"Give him a break, Joy," I murmur.

"Stay out of it, Hopeless."

I cringe some more. I hate it when she calls me that. "He's trying, at least."

"He's a useless prick is what he is." Joy jumbles all the dishes together in a manner that gives away the fact that she was also a waitress for years. She storms into the kitchen. "You hear that, Bruce?"

Bruce places both hands on the counter, stares at the floor and sighs as Joy shuts the door and rips into him for being a general all-round screwup.

Daisy bounces from couch to chair to my

lap to the floor and then starts her circuit all over again. I can barely look at her. Whenever I do, all I can think of is my vastly empty wallet. That money was all I had. I'd given the rest to the Larchberry Thailand Project. Sure, it's great to be charitable, and sure, I have it better than most of the world, but right now I'd give anything for just two dollars to get on the subway and go somewhere interesting to get away from the train wreck that is Joy and Bruce.

While Joy verbally dissects Bruce in the kitchen, I slip out with Daisy and head for Prospect Park. Huge and free and green and treed, with trails and meadows and a lake that you can't swim in. This will be my summer solace. The last time I was in Brooklyn, with my parents for one of Joy's performances, I spent most of my time here. And this summer, with not a penny to my name, my options are limited. Daisy finds some off-leash dogs to torment, and I find a patch of shade under a tree. Everything starts to feel a little more manageable.

There's a kite festival going on across the meadow, so I lie down and watch the box kites and stunt kites and regular kites soar against the cloudless sky. Peaceful, but only until the thoughts creep back, the ones I'd promised myself I wouldn't entertain, like why my parents wouldn't let me stay at Larchberry for the summer.

"It's not that we don't trust you," Dad had said. "It's just that we were seventeen once too." He took my mother's hand. "We fell in love when we were seventeen, after all."

"I'm not in love with Orion, and I'm definitely not going to have his love child." Orion had been a mistake—a total and utter mistake. "It's over with him."

Until Orion came along, they were going to let me stay home for the summer. My parents might be hippies, but they might as well be born-again Christians when it comes to their little girl having sex. Summer at Larchberry brings a flock of Woofers—Workers on Organic Farms. Tanned and fit, they come to help with the crops and the market. Virginity doesn't last long at Larchberry, whether the parentals acknowledge it or not.

I was fifteen my first time—he was a seventeen-year-old, staunchly vegan surfer boy from our sister commune in California. His name was Denver, and I'd managed to keep him and the two others secret from my parents. Just my luck, they had to find out about Orion.

Mistake number one: he's twenty-four. Mistake number two: my parents caught us smoking hash. Mistake number three: we were naked at the time, in a makeshift bed in the hayloft. Mistake number four: there was a used condom flung and hanging like a flag from a rake at my parents' eye level. Mistake number five: he's married. But I didn't know that! I didn't!

"I'm not Joy," I protested. "I'm not going to disappear for two years and come back with a drug problem and various STDs. We're two different people."

"We have your best interests at heart, love," Dad said.

"So you're going to send me to the one who

did disappear for two years and came back with a drug problem and various STDs?"

"Joy has done a lot of growing up since then," Dad said.

"Not that much," I muttered.

"Say what you have to say clearly," my mom said. "The phrase is 'speak your mind,' not 'mumble' it."

"I don't want to go to New York for the summer. I want to stay here," I said.

"That's not an option."

"So you're going to blame me for Joy's screwups—"

"Language, sweetheart," they said in unison.

"You two met at seventeen and had Joy when you were still seventeen and you're still together, doesn't that count for something?"

They gazed lovingly at each other for a second and then returned their attentions to me. "Seventeen is a vulnerable and empowering time in one's life…" Dad said.

"…you struggle between the freedom of some independence and the restraints of the expectations and concerns of the people who love you very much," my mom finished for them both.

And so here I am in Prospect Park, watching the kites overhead, instead of working the farm with the Woofers, with bonfires and drumming after dark, skinny-dipping in the river, and sweet, hot, high afternoons picking blueberries.

My parents are such hypocrites. They smoke pot all the time. And they always did, too, even when I was little. My mother even dared to say, but only once, that it's because she smoked pot while she was pregnant that we turned out so mellow. She said that before Joy disappeared for two years and returned with a drug problem. Mom swears she never said it now. Now she's all about the Stay Away From Drugs speeches, while all the while I know she's got a stash in her purse at any given time, unless we're crossing the border.

Daisy comes romping back on her short little legs, followed by a big yellow mutt with a studded collar.

"Hey, dogs." The yellow dog flops onto his back for some loving. Daisy clambers all over him, nipping at him playfully. I look around for whoever might be with the yellow dog. "Go on, get out of here." The dog rolls over and sits up. He finds a stick and drops it in my lap. I stand, pick up the stick and try to figure out who in the hundreds of people might belong to him. I can't decide, so I throw the stick in the direction of the thickest swell of people. "Go find your human. And don't come back!"

He fetches the stick, races back to me and drops it at my feet.

"Who do you belong to?" His tag has a phone number and a name. "Clocker?"

He barks and wags his tail.

"Well, go on, Clocker." I wander toward the crowd, dogs in tow. "Find your human."

Clocker trots happily at my side and shows no interest in anyone else.

"Great." I look around for a Lost & Found tent or somewhere I can leave him. The kite festival people tell me that they won't take him because of the risk to kids. "Whatever you say." As we speak, Clocker is on his back, wriggling with delight, getting his belly rubbed by a hoard of rambunctious children.

I find a park employee, but he suggests the pound, and I don't like that idea.

"You phoned the number yet?" the park guy asks.

"I don't have a quarter."

"Cell phone?"

I shake my head. He gives me a quarter and wishes me luck. I find a pay phone and dial the number. It's a Brooklyn number, and after a couple of rings it goes to voice mail. A girl's voice, and without a New Yorker accent.

"You've reached Nat. Leave me a message here or not, but if you've found Clocker, please, please, please don't take him to the pound. I can't afford to keep bailing him out of there. Leave your cell number and I'll hook up with you right away. Thanks, and rock on, crouton."

It beeps. "Uh, yeah, hi," I say. "I've got Clocker, but I don't have a cell, and I can't remember my sister's cell and I don't know where I am in the park, so…" Clocker barks, as if on cue. "So I guess I'll head up to the gardens and wait there for a while." I hang up. "So, dogs," Clocker and Daisy wag their tails. "Guess we're stuck with each other for a while."

I wait at the gardens for almost two hours, until I think even Joy will start to worry, which isn't something that comes naturally to her. I've been gone half the day by now. Both dogs have finally tired each other out with all of their you're-my-new-best-friend romping and are now collapsed in panting heaps at my feet. I'm getting hungry. This whole broke thing is not going to work for me. Not only do I not have any money to get anything to eat, I don't even have a quarter to call Clocker's exceptionally irresponsible human again.

I'll have to take Clocker back to Joy's place. That won't go over well. She's got the urban hipster thing going on—minimalist and very clean, with select, expensive, breakable items at Clocker's tail-wagging height. And Joy hates dogs. We had such a battle over

Daisy coming. I might have been less than impressed when Orion presented her to me as an apology for lying, but now I love her to neurons, and I'd never leave her for that long.

The elevator is on the fritz, so we hike up six flights of stairs at what has got to be the hottest time of the day. Daisy conks out at the third floor, so I carry her the rest of the way. And then, the minute we get in the door, and before I can dog-proof the place, Clocker waggles across the living room and sends a blown-glass sphere smashing onto the floor. The noise summons Bruce and Joy from the bedroom, each wrapped in a sheet and bleary-eyed from sleep or who knows what else.

Joy kneels and gingerly picks up a shard. "You know how much this cost?"

"Add it to my bill." I hold the dogs back. "Can you clean it up?" The last thing I need is another vet bill for sliced-up paws.

"Not a chance, Hopeless." She drops the piece. "And what the hell is that dog doing here?"

While Bruce sweeps up the glass, I tell her.

"You're here, what, like a few hours?" she asks. "How can you even get up to this much shit?" She disappears into the bedroom, still talking. "You keep it up at this rate and I'm so sending you home."

"And you would so be The Unforgiven," I call back.

"Get rid of the dog," she says as she reemerges, dressed in a strapless sundress and high heels. "By the time we get back."

"Where are you going?"

"Bruce has an audition in Manhattan."

"You're coming with me?" Bruce beams. "That's so sweet, honey."

"I'm meeting Cecily for lunch, Bruce." Joy doctors her lipstick at the mirror by the door. "I told you that."

"Yeah, you did." Poor Bruce. He actually slumps. Why does he stay with her? Even if it's for sex, is it really worth it? "We'll hook up after?" he asks.

"It's a girl thing, Bruce," Joy says.

"We can get together later, Bruce," I offer.

"If you want." It's not like hanging out with Bruce is at the top of my To Do list, but I feel sorry for him, after all. Us hippie kids are supposed to end up with more than our fair share of compassion, but apparently Joy left hers at Larchberry.

"Yeah?" He beams again. He's more like a puppy than Daisy, really. He tries so hard. "You want to get dinner somewhere? We can get ice cream at Uncle Louie G's after. Butter pecan, remember that?"

"Yeah, the best—"

"God," Joy cuts me off as she slings her purse over her shoulder.

"What?" Bruce says, wounded.

"You're going to hang out with my baby sister on a Saturday night?"

"It's her first night here. Why not?"

"Your social doom, baby." She kisses him on the cheek. "Call me?"

"Are you going to meet us later?"

"We'll see what everyone's up to." With that she flounces out of the apartment, high heels clicking toward the elevator.

I smile. "Elevator's dead."

Even Bruce, ever the doormat, smiles as a faint "Shit!" resounds down the hall before the door to the stairwell slams shut.

Chapter Four

People in New York City don't have real phones. Bruce and Joy each have a cell, which they take with them when they leave, which leaves me with no phone. So I have to scrounge for a quarter because I didn't think to call Clocker's exceptionally irresponsible owner while there were two cell phones in the house. I take the dogs and the stairs to the street and find a pay phone and update Nat's voice mail with Joy's address.

About an hour later, the buzzer rings. I lift the receiver and see her in the intercom camera. The black-and-white grainy image makes her look like some kind of hoodlum.

"You're Clocker's human?" I ask.

"Yeah, hi." She puts her hands, prayer like, to her chin. "Thank you, thank you, thank you!"

"It's about time."

"Sorry." She puts her face right up to the camera so she's all lip ring and wide eyes. "You're my hero?"

"I'll bring him down," I say.

"Wait! I really, really have to pee." She does a little jig. "Can I come up?"

"You expect me to let a perfect stranger in? This is New York!"

"My dog's great, isn't he?" She eyeballs the camera again. "I named him Clocker because his tail wags in a perfect circle, did you notice? Isn't he the best? They say pets take after their owners. What do you say? I look harmless, right? Come on, I'm dying down here."

I can appreciate the need for a decent place

to pee in Brooklyn. I've been there myself. "Just for a minute." I buzz her in. Let's hope she's not a serial killer cleverly disguised as some blond-dreadlocked skater girl.

I open the door and Clocker barges down the hall to greet her as she emerges from the stairs, not at all out of breath.

"There's my boy!" Nat drops to her knees and hugs him. He's wagging his tail so hard he practically shimmies across the tile.

"Where you been, Mister Bad?" Clocker hurtles himself gleefully onto his back and she scratches his belly. "You went to the park without me? Did you see all your buddies?"

"And where were you?" I say, hands on my hips. I feel suddenly parental, which I don't like, so I drop my hands.

"Work." She stands up. "Thanks for looking after him."

She's taller than me, lankier too, with skinny hips and long tanned legs. Her dreads poke out from under a blue bandana. She's got an eyebrow ring too, I can see now, and a tattoo of what looks like a bike chain and a series of gears climbing up her arm. She might be my age, maybe a little older. She'd fit right in as a Woofer. Her hands are just as dirty, and she's as tanned and as freaky looking as any of them.

"Grease." She holds her hands up. "Bicycles. Clocker comes to work with me. He usually stays put, but every once in a while he takes off to the park without me. It's okay, though." She hugs him again. "You always find your way back to me, don't you, Mister Bad?"

"With a little help," I say.

"Hell, that's what humans are for, aren't they? Helping each other?" She touches her hand to her heart and bows slightly. I can't tell if she's being sarcastic or sincere. Being raised by hippies makes me a little gullible at times. "And I thank you. I really, truly thank you. Now, can I use your can?"

I step aside and she beelines for the bathroom. As she comes out, she does up her fly and checks out the living room. "Nice place."

"It's my sister's."

"Yeah?" She picks up a hunk of metal

Joy calls art. "Let me guess. Late twenties, wishes she was living in Manhattan. Probably a little…" She puts a finger to her nose and sniffs.

"Bang on."

"Can spot 'em a mile away." She sets the sculpture down. "I'm Nat, by the way."

"Hope."

"I cleaned my hands. Or they're a little better anyway. See?" She holds them up for inspection before we shake. "Well, thanks again, Hope."

Her grip is firm and warm and she holds onto my hand for almost as long as Maira did on the plane. Maybe it's a Brooklyn thing. She's kind of gazing at me, in a weird way. Another weird thing—a really weird thing—is that I don't want her to let go.

"So, Hope." She lets go. "See you around?"

I nod, not sure what to say. She whistles for Clocker, who's curled up on Joy's very expensive chaise lounge, and they leave. I shake my head at Daisy, who's whining at the door, already missing her new buddy.

"What was that?" I ask, completely bewildered. Daisy lies down, nose touching the door, and whines. "Just exactly what was *that*?"

Chapter Five

Today is day six of my job at the vet's, and I haven't seen Nat since. I've been walking the dogs first thing each morning, and then again in the evenings, and keeping an eye out for her the whole time, although I'm not sure why. Thomas, the vet, is really easy to work for, thank the Universe for that. He's mellow and reminds me of Dad a little, except he has opera blaring all day, and Dad would play folk music, or jazz, but definitely not opera. This is also day six of Joy's slavery schedule of housework and errands I have to do to pay off the broken glass thingy. I'm in the middle of alphabetizing her bookshelf when Maira calls.

"I need you!" She says, frantic. "My nanny just quit! Come for supper tomorrow night?"

She offers me a nannying job, which is fantastic, but even if she hadn't, I've been so lonely I'd go just for the company. She needs me for four days a week, she explains, while she goes to her job as an editor at a publisher in Manhattan. So tomorrow I'll get to meet the guy she'd been so upset about on the plane.

Maira's address is a brownstone on Garfield, just below the park and the trendy shops. There's a tiny, neat, lush garden out front, and flowers spilling out of pots lining the steps, leading to a red front door and an antique doorbell. From what I can see from the skinny window beside the door, Maira is rich, rich, rich. There's just no other word for it. Or her husband is. Or they both are. Classy furniture, walls of books, tasteful art and just a glimpse of a kitchen that looks like it sprang fully formed from the loins of the *How Cool People Live Guidebook*.

Maira comes to the door, a twin on each hip. She manages to unlock and open the door in a way only a mother of infant twins could.

"Am I ever glad to see you." She offers me one. "Felix," she says, just as I was going to guess he was Avery. "Come on in, I'll give you a tour."

It takes less than a minute before I decide that when I have a home of my own, I want it to be just like hers. Never mind the higgledy-piggledy, homemade, wood-smoke, comforting jumble of Larchberry Farm. I vote for this—smart and artful and eclectic and interesting and tidy, but still really lived-in and human and warm. She shows me the kitchen last. We park ourselves there, and Maira starts concocting a marinade for the three lamb chops sitting raw and ugly on a white platter.

Why don't people plan something vegetarian when they have a dinner guest they don't know? Why does the vegetarian always have to be the one who ruins the menu? I'm just about to tell her that I'm a vegetarian, when the front door opens.

"Hey there!" a woman calls down the hall. "Where are those beautiful blue-eyed boys?"

"More company?" I ask.

"My partner, Larissa."

Oh, okay. I need a private little minute with that piece of information. So there's no *he* at all? Well, of course they're lesbians, because she surely doesn't mean "business partner," not judging by the kiss Larissa lays on her, dipping her like a ballroom dancer.

"Larissa, this is Hope. She's saving our collective ass, so supper is in her honor. Crack a bottle of that Riesling, will you?"

Lesbians. Okay. Not a big deal. There were a couple of dykes who lived at the farm for a while. And then there's Kyle, the old gay guy who shoes the horses, but other than that and the odd queer Woofer, I don't know

47

many people like...like *that*. Larchberry is all Man-shall-work-the-fields-and-build-things-and-repair-all-that-breaks, while Woman-shall-also-work-the-fields-and-raise-babies-and-cook-and-clean-and-sew, and then together we shall smoke pot and sing folk songs and let our babies run around naked.

Larissa hands me a glass of wine. "Are you old enough to drink?"

"I told you, she's a hippie kid." Maira gives her a peck on the cheek. They don't look like lesbians. But then, I don't know what lesbians look like, except for the two at the farm, who just looked like each other: miserable, each with a long, dirty braid and a big butt. "You've had wine before, haven't you?"

"Lots." I nod. "We make it at the farm. Blueberry wine."

Why, I wonder, do I have the urge to bolt out the door and never come back? I'm not against queers or anything. That isn't it. Larchberry might be isolated, but it is as left wing as it gets, and all the parents work really hard to raise us as liberal freethinkers.

I have no problem with diversity, don't get me wrong, but it's like a heavy, unpleasant weight has parked in my stomach. Orion pops into my mind, and thinking about him always makes me squirmy. He was such a mistake. I try to think of something else, like picking blueberries, but instead I get a flash of one of the nights in the barn, with the candles and the blueberry wine. I cannot believe he lied to me about being married and then thought that giving me a puppy would make it all better.

"I missed you," Maira says. She and Larissa kiss full on, and I get those sexy butterflies in my belly along with a flash of Orion and me kissing on the bluff above the river just before we're about to jump in. Do I miss him? Is that what this is about? How can I miss him? He was all wrong. Maybe I'm just lonely. Well, not *maybe*. Am. I *am* lonely.

Maira goes back to preparing supper, and Larissa gets onto the floor with the babies, who are not quite crawling on a sheepskin rug in a patch of sunlight. The whole scene is like an ad for hardwood flooring in one of those posh interior design magazines. I sit with my wine and wish I could go home. Not to Joy's, but to Larchberry. I've had enough of Brooklyn and enough of me. I don't get myself these days. I'm my very own stranger. And I miss everybody, mostly my parents. But even if I went home, they wouldn't be there.

"So tell us how your visit's been so far," Maira says as she tops up my wine.

When I finish telling them, they're both staring at me, wide eyes all sympathetic.

"It sounds awful. Do you want to stay here?" Maira points at the ceiling. "We have a million spare rooms up there."

"Thanks, but I've got my sister."

"But it sounds like a nightmare!" Maira tucks the lamb into the oven. "And I'm sorry, but *she* sounds like a nightmare." My brain is so tired right now; I just don't feel like telling her I'm a vegetarian. "You're sleeping on a couch. That's just not right."

"Did you show her the nanny suite?" Larissa says.

"We didn't do the third floor, no."

"Come on," Larissa says as she tops up our wine. "I'll show you."

The rooms are beautiful, of course. There's a small bedroom and a sitting room and a little bathroom with a claw-foot tub and Victorian photographs of nude women on the walls.

"What do you think?" Larissa leans in the doorway, arms crossed. I can't look at her, and I'm not sure why. Maybe because I'm more weirded out by the whole lesbian thing than I think? Or maybe because the photograph above her shoulder is rather suggestive. I wonder what the other nanny thought about all of this. Maybe it's why she left.

"It's all yours," Larissa says. "If you want."

"I don't know."

And I don't. I'm supposed to be under the watchful eye of Joy, but I've hardly seen her since I got off the plane. There's never any food to eat at Joy's, and I still don't have any money, and Thomas brings me a bagel and coffee every morning because he thinks I'm starving to death. And sleeping on the couch does suck, especially because Joy and Bruce usually crash through the door near dawn, a loud drunken duo. And then Joy always calls Cecily and rehashes their entire evening—which they've just spent together—at the top of her lungs while perched on the edge of the very couch I'm trying to sleep on. The bed in the nanny suite is huge and pillowed and looks ever so sleepable.

"Well, it's not going anywhere." Larissa sits on the bed. "It's yours any time." She leans back, her hands on the bedspread. Suddenly I remember Orion and me on the four-poster in his room in the Big House. What is that about? I blush.

"I'll keep it in mind." I back toward the door. "Uh, thanks for the offer."

The boys fell asleep while we were upstairs, so we tiptoe as we put supper out. The table set and candles lit—even though it's not dark—Maira sits down and fills a plate with lamb and lemon rice and grilled asparagus and salad and hands it to me. I've had enough wine by now and am so perplexed by myself that I just hold the plate and stare at it instead of taking it and strategically pushing the meat around, which is my usual tactic when confronted with dead animals on my plate.

"Something the matter?" Larissa asks.

"Sort of. I don't eat meat."

"Oh, sweetheart, why didn't you say so?" Maira takes the plate. "I have a perfectly good block of tofu in the fridge. I could've done something with it."

"Sorry."

Maira gives the plate to Larissa.

"I was going to say something and then I just didn't. I don't know why." I shake my head. "It's weird."

"What's weird?" Maira fills another plate.

"Everything, to be honest."

Maira sets the meatless wonder in front of me. She and Larissa look at each other with one of those "couple" looks. I guess lesbians have those too.

"Are you still interested in working for us?" Maira asks.

"Yes! It's just that I—" It's just that what?

It's just that I'm having a panic attack right here at the supper table? My fingers are tingly, and a cold rush climbs my spine, settling into an icy ache across my skull, just like when Orion finally told me about his wife. His *wife*!

"Is it because we're queer?" Larissa's voice is deliberately even.

I close my eyes. That is part of it, my guts tell me so, but that's not all of it. "I think I'm just homesick." Uh-oh. The tears are preparing for mass exodus.

"She's probably tired too," Maira says, "sleeping on that couch every night..."

"...if she's managing to sleep at all, poor thing," Larissa says.

The way they finish each other's sentences makes me miss my parents all the more. I want to have one of my mom's earth mama hugs, and I want my dad to talk to. He always helps me sort out what my panic attacks are about. What would he say about this one? I'm not sure that I want to know. Something tells me this is a biggie.

"I just wish I could talk to my parents."

The tears let loose. "I just miss them so much!"

Larissa and Maira share another look, and then Maira takes my wineglass and offers me a tissue instead. "Do you want us to take you home?"

"Home?" That, of course, makes me cry harder. "That's just it. I want to go to my *real* home."

Larissa rubs my back, which for some reason reminds me of how she'd patted the bedspread earlier, which makes me think of Orion again. *What* is going on? All of this is so confusing. "Do you want to go to your sister's?"

I shake my head.

"Do you want to stay here for the night, upstairs?"

I nod. "But I have to go get Daisy."

"Her dog," Maira replies to Larissa's look.

"Okay. All of this is manageable." Larissa stands. "Come on. We'll go get Daisy with the car."

Larissa drives me back to Joy's and waits

in the street, double-parked, while I drag myself up the six flights of stairs because the elevator is busted again. No one is home, as usual. I pack a bag, collect Daisy and her food and leave Joy and Bruce a note.

On the drive back we are stopped in traffic in front of Uncle Louie G's. There's Nat, talking with a girl behind the counter, while Clocker begs beside her. Nat pays for a cone and then gives the whole thing to Clocker, ice cream and all. She sees us and waves. I'm instantly all nerves.

"Larissa, hey!"

Larissa pulls the car over. I'm acutely aware of my red-rimmed eyes and snotty nose and general miserableness. "You staying out of trouble, Nat?"

"Of course I am." Nat leans into Larissa's window and sees me. "Oh, hi."

"Hi." I really don't want anyone to see me like this, and, for some reason, especially not her. Daisy clambers over Larissa and slobbers all over Clocker, who's stuck his smelly mug in the window.

"Thanks for the other day," Nat says. "I really appreciated it."

"No big deal." I wish Larissa would put the gas pedal to use. "No problem."

"Nat?" Larissa says in a singsong. "What's going on?"

"She found Clocker the other day. That's all." Nat backs away, hands up. "Hey, I am staying out of trouble."

"Good." Larissa looks at me, then back at Nat. "Good to hear, Nat. Take care."

Larissa drives, silent until she's circled their block twice, looking for a parking spot. "So, you've met Nat."

"Sort of."

"She's a piece of Park Slope color, you could say. Her and Clocker. Clocker wanders off so much everyone knows to look out for him and bring him back to the bike shop."

"No one seemed to know him the other day in the park."

"Well, not *everybody*. You know what I mean."

I shrug. "Whatever."

"She's a good kid."

I shrug again.

"She'd make a good friend for someone who might be in the market for one," she says as she parallel parks in an impossibly small spot. "Do you want me to call her? Invite her over?"

"No!" I gather my things and fling open the door. "No, thanks, I mean. I'm okay. You don't need to do that. Really."

Part of me wishes she would, though. But the problem is that the weight in my stomach, the butterflies and the nerves have all sculpted themselves into one big thunk of a realization: I have a crush on Nat. A crush on a *girl*.

Chapter Six

Crush or not, I hardly have time to think about it. I don't want to anyway, so I am thankful that a day with the twins is life in fast-forward times two. "Handful" does not even begin to describe it. Four whole days go by before I have a chance to sit still for more than a minute. I'm all about distractions, anyway. If I keep myself busy hanging out with the babies, walking the dogs at the vet, losing myself for entire hours in the little garden, I don't have to figure out the Nat thing. Besides, I'm sure it'll pass.

That Saturday, Maira and Larissa invite me to come along with them to the beach the next morning, but I've gone from lonely to human overload, so I decline in favor of a day by myself. Daisy and I go to walk the dogs first. I've paid off my bill, but I still walk the dogs as a favor for Thomas.

"Your sister was in here looking for you," Thomas tells me in place of a "hello."

"She knows where I've been." I gather the leashes.

"I don't think so," Thomas says. "She was pretty frantic. I told her you're nannying, but I didn't know the details. She wants you to call her." Thomas hands me the phone. "Immediately."

Joy is obviously hungover and obviously furious. "There is no note!" she screams at me when I tell her I'd left one. Her voice is groggy and scratchy. "You are such a liar!"

"There's a note, Joy." I take a deep breath. "I left it on the table, under the window."

"What the hell…" I can tell Joy is getting out of bed to go look. "You are in big shit, kiddo. Mom and Dad called—"

"They did? How are they?"

"Well, understandably upset when I told them I had no clue where you were."

"But I left you a note!"

"And here it is." Joy laughs. "Right where you said it was. Huh. Go figure. Maybe you could've stuck it on the mirror or the door or a cupboard or something where we would've actually found it."

"I can't believe you told them that!" I put a hand to my forehead. "What did they say?"

"They canned the project." Joy coughs. "They're coming home to look for their precious little runaway."

"But I didn't run away!" I don't believe this! They must be dying with worry over there! "I got a job and a real bed to sleep in! Some people would call that responsible."

Joy laughs again, which makes her cough some more. When she recovers from her hacking fit, she covers the phone and mumbles something to Bruce. At least,

I assume it's Bruce. With her you never know.

"Oh, Hopeless," she says and then starts laughing again. "I didn't tell them, are you kidding? I told them you were out. They're going to call back on Tuesday morning. It was a joke. Ha, ha, you know?"

"You are such a bitch, Joy."

"Ooo, hippie kid goes nasty." Joy's laugh turns into a cackle. "Call the press!"

"I'm hanging up now, and the only reason I'm telling you that is so you can't say I hung up on you."

"Beat you to it!" Joy screeches and slams the phone down.

I walk the dogs and then take Daisy up to the park. The whole while, I'm seething. Joy absolutely cannot be my parents' child. She must be a foundling, some evil demon spawn from wretched origins best forgotten. I let Daisy off her leash and lie down in a piece of shade to feel sorry for myself. Not a minute passes before Daisy comes charging back with Clocker hot on her heels. I sit up and scan the meadow. No dreadlocked tattooed crush on the horizon. I don't know if I'm relieved or disappointed.

"Here we go again." I lie back down. "Get comfy, guys. I'm not doing anything about it in any hurry." About Clocker or the crush.

Before I know it, and without meaning to, I fall asleep. When I wake up, the sun is significantly higher in the sky and neither Clocker nor Daisy is in sight. I leap up.

"Daisy!" I spin around. A million off-leash dogs, but no scrappy little Westie with a big yellow boyfriend. "Clocker!"

How could I have fallen asleep? So far, this summer is about as hellish as it gets. No Larchberry, no parents, a crush on a girl—which does not compute—no money, a useless sister, and now I've lost my dog in New York City! This is my time to shine, apparently. Worse, Daisy is one of the breeds people steal to sell. I take a deep breath and bend over, my hands on my knees, feeling that familiar chill of panic flood over me. I couldn't even begin to pinpoint what this one's about. There's so much to choose from.

Where to begin with the spectacular mess that is me?

"Calm down, Hope." I swear the ground is moving beneath my feet. I sit down, but I still feel dizzy. "It's going to be okay," I tell myself. "Count to ten, nice and slow." I do.

"Now get up and look for the dogs." I force myself to stand. "I can do this. I can." I scan the horizon. "Daisy! Clocker!"

I cross the meadow, calling for them, all the while sick with worry. Daisy has no idea how to survive in the city, with all the traffic and people and peril everywhere. What are the chances she'd actually end up safe and sound in the pound and I'd find her?

I'm just about to give up when I hear someone call my name.

It's Nat, on her bike, with Clocker bounding ahead of her.

"Have you seen Daisy?" I run toward her.

"Yeah, she's with me."

And she is, a muddy, panting mess in the crate behind Nat's seat, half asleep.

"Where have you been?" I pick her up

and hug her, mud and all. She licks my face. "Where'd you go?"

"I found them at the other end of the park, terrorizing the ducks."

I set Daisy on the grass, where she promptly lies down and is soon snoring.

"Thanks, Nat," I say.

"Even?" Nat gets off her bike. Both she and Clocker are muddy too.

"What do you mean?" I ask.

"Come on, admit it." Nat cocks her head. "You thought I was an idiot for losing my dog. Right?"

"Yeah. I did." Clocker flops down on the grass too. "Even."

A birthday party bustles in a stretch of shade nearby. The children attack a piñata that swings from a low branch. A couple more whacks and it bursts, and after they scramble for the candy, the flock of frilly-dressed girls comes running over, squealing in Spanish.

The mothers holler at them, and then Nat says something in Spanish and the girls stop short of the filthy dogs and turn in their party shoes and head back to the adults.

"They wanted to play with the dogs," Nat says. "But they would've gotten filthy."

"You speak Spanish?"

"Yeah." Nat stretches her arms over her head, pulling her muscles taut. She has yummy muscles, like a Woofer. Universe? What the hell am I thinking?

Nat's saying something, but I hardly hear her. Her legs are super long and extra muscled, from all the biking, no doubt. And completely filthy. "Whatcha looking at?"

"Your legs are covered in mud."

"I had to fish Daisy out of the marsh. She wouldn't come when I called." Nat drags a finger along her muddy calf and I just about swoon. This is nuts. Completely nuts! Since when did I become queer?

"Come to think of it," Nat says, "you might owe me."

Get a grip, Hope. "I don't think so," I manage to say. "If you remember, I spent the entire day with Clocker." I put my hands on my hips and shake my head. "And Daisy is filthy."

"That's not my fault!"

"Still, I can't take her back to Maira's like this."

"You're staying with them?"

"Yeah, long story."

"They must have a hose," Nat says. "Let's go turn it on them. You can tell me on the way."

Nat makes me nervous, and when I'm nervous I talk a mile a minute and leave out tons of stuff, so it only takes a block to tell her how I ended up staying with Maira and Larissa. The story over, I have nothing left to say and I'm practically paralyzed with nerves.

"Want to go ahead with your bike?" I suggest. "I'll meet you there?"

"Nah." She glances at me out of the corner of her eye. "I'm enjoying the company."

I glance up at the sky. Universe, if you have power at all, help me to not act like a babbling, confused idiot.

The two of us, Nat's bike and Clocker—Daisy's riding in the basket—take up the whole sidewalk. People have to step into the street to walk around us, but I don't care. Apparently this crush has obliterated my manners. Thankfully, Nat fills the gaps, telling me about the neighborhood.

"That used to be an armory, but now it's a homeless shelter."

"The guy who lives there played drums for Elvis."

"There was an ecstasy lab in there, but it got busted." And so on, little bits of Brooklyn filling my awkwardness like confetti.

We go through the garden gate, and as soon as Nat turns on the hose, Daisy dashes under the porch, getting even dirtier. Clocker puts up with it, his tail between his legs and his head hung low, but he lets her rinse him off.

"You do this often?"

"Often enough."

Daisy, on the other hand, will not come out from under the porch.

"Come on, Daisy." I try treats and begging, but she cowers in the farthest corner and lets out a belligerent little bark every once in a while. "Get out of there!"

Nat gets on her knees just inches away from me. "I'll go get her."

"I wouldn't bother." I am keenly aware of how little space there is between us. "She'll come out when she's ready."

"I don't mind." Nat shimmies under the porch. "I'm already dirty." After a little dodge dog and a whole lot of yapping, she grabs Daisy's scruff and drags her out.

"Look at you now," I say. "You're totally filthy!"

"Yep." Nat yanks at her grimy tank top. "I'm one dirty girl."

"You need hosing off more than Daisy."

She raises an eyebrow and grins. "So go for it."

Okay, now that is totally a come-on!

"I didn't…I don't—" I pick up Daisy. If she were a guy, I'd flirt back, but a girl? How do I know she even likes girls? Don't be stupid, Hopeless. She's about as dykey as it gets. But what do you do with a girl? That thought makes me blush even more. "I should give Daisy a bath. I'll use the sink in the basement. Do you—?"

"Do I—"

"I wasn't—"

"Wasn't what?" Nat cocks her head, grin still in place.

I laugh, the high nervous laugh Joy loves to mock. I am officially losing it. Any minute now I am going to morph into an immature, stuttering, laughing mess who doesn't know if I want to kiss a girl for the first time in my life or if I want to run, screaming, into traffic. Getting smacked by a yellow cab might be just what I need. Nothing like a couple of busted legs to force yourself to figure things out. Seriously, I'm considering it.

Nat's still grinning. I bet she's getting off on making me squirm. "How about I go home and have a shower?" Yes! Go! Before I humiliate myself! She grabs her bike. "You want me to go?"

"I think so. Yeah." I cling to Daisy and nod robotically. "Okay. Sounds good. You go. Yeah, good idea."

Nat whistles for Clocker. "Bye?"

Apparently I'm stupefied, because all I can do is nod.

"And then Hope says, 'Bye, Nat.'" Nat laughs.

Isn't she fazed by any of this? Does she do this all the time? Make unsuspecting, seemingly straight girls squirm? Or am I making it all up? But making up *what*? The butterflies are real. The fact that I want to kiss her is real. But what I felt about Orion and the other boys was real too, wasn't it?

Would kissing a girl be different from kissing boys? If all I did was kiss her, would that make me queer? Are you queer just for thinking it? Or does doing it make you queer? And what if I don't want to be queer? Do I get a say in this at all?

Nat and Clocker disappear out the gate while I am pinned in place by questions. I stand there, stunned, and then I creep along the side of the house and watch them make their way down the sidewalk, Nat on her bike, Clocker trailing behind her. Nat rears up and pops a wheelie. It seems triumphant, like she knows something I don't.

Does she? I almost run after her to ask, but then Clocker looks back, and I duck back into the yard, as if he might tell Nat that I was spying on her.

Chapter Seven

Larissa and Maira come home as it gets dark. When I hear the key in the front door, I race upstairs and hide in the stairwell and listen to their quiet murmurs as they bring in the sleeping twins and all the beach gear and baby bags and coolers. I should go down to help, but I don't know what to say to them, and I know that if I start talking, I won't stop. I know that I'd end up telling them about Orion, which makes me feel crappy just thinking about it, and then, worse, about Nat, which I just plain don't understand. I think it'd be best if I just didn't say anything. I don't trust myself right now. Hell, I don't even know myself right now. Thankfully, I'd planned ahead and left them a note on the counter in the kitchen saying I was going to bed early.

I try watching TV, but entire shows run by and I don't even notice. I turn the TV off and crawl into bed, but all I can think about is Nat, standing there in the sunlight, her head cocked, and that grin. I stuff my head under my pillow. What am I thinking? What am I doing? Do I want to kiss Nat just to say I'd kissed a girl? Is it because I'm staying with lesbians? Not that I think it is catching—that's ridiculous—but it's not like the thought had ever occurred to me before now. Something is happening, and I don't know what. Yeah, it could be that I'm into girls, but it could also just be me doing what I often do, which is doing something for the sake of experience. My dad has warned me more than once that while he supports my insatiable curiosity, he worries that it might get me into a bit of trouble here and there. I think this is a fine example of "here and there."

I chuck the pillow across the room and get out of bed. There's no way I can sleep! How can anyone actually sleep when life is going on?

I look at myself in the mirror. Am I queer? Do I want to be a lesbian? Do I care either way? I wish I could call my parents. Dad would know what to do. I shut my eyes and put my fingers to my temples. When I was little, my dad and I would try to guess what the other was thinking. Okay, not only when I was little—we still do it, as hokey as it sounds. It's pretty amazing how often we're right. One of us will tell Mom a number we're thinking of, or a picture we have in mind, and lots of times we get it right. Mind you, way more times we're completely wrong.

"Dad?" I whisper. "Can you hear me?"

Nothing. Maybe Thailand is just too far away.

"There's this girl…" I open my eyes. This is stupid. I know what he'd say. That part is easy. *Follow your heart, baby girl.* I'm one of those super blessed kids who have parents who would actually celebrate if their kid wanted to join the circus or become a tattoo artist or sing in a rock band or make pottery for a living, so kissing a girl is nothing they'd have a problem with. In fact, The Talk in our house included stuff like: "It's okay to love women if you're a woman, or men if you're a man...the Universe creates love of all kinds, and all of it is pure and beautiful and precious."

I should've kissed her. How else am I going to know?

"Damn," I mutter at my reflection. "Now you might not get another chance. Way to go, Hopeless."

Sleep is like an impatient slip of nothing, but for some reason I wake up and the world feels like one big blue ball of brilliance. I bounce downstairs, scoop a baby up in each arm and dance them around the kitchen to the music from the radio.

"Why the good mood?" Larissa stares

bleary-eyed at the coffeemaker as it slowly does its thing.

"Not sure." I set Felix down, grab a mug from the cupboard and pour Larissa a cup of coffee mid-brew. "Ta da!"

"Wow." Larissa grips the mug. "How did you do that?"

"It has a sensor." I laugh. "You didn't know that?"

"No." Larissa takes a sip. "Oh, yes. That's it. Bless you, Hope."

Felix flaps his hands at me, so I pick him up, perch him on my hip and get busy mashing bananas one-handed. I'm getting good at it. Maira comes into the kitchen, cell phone to her ear.

"Not acceptable," she says in her work tone, which is way different from her mommy tone. She gestures at Larissa. "Categorically not."

Larissa pulls a snack-size yogurt out of the fridge and hands it to her.

Thank you, Maira mouths. *Love you.* "And I'm equally confident that you heard me the first time. The answer is no." She kisses

Larissa on the cheek, nuzzles each baby and manages to keep the phone call going the whole time as she heads for the door.

"Man, I love that woman!" Larissa says as Maira leaves. "Amazing, isn't she?"

"Yep." A couple of days after I moved in, Maira mentioned that she'd been out west dealing with her parents, who were splitting up after forty-two years together. That's what the whole emotional mess on the plane was about. Apparently an argument over organic strawberries was the last straw for her dad, but I'm guessing the mistress of thirteen years was a contributing factor too. Anyway, the point is, Maira and Larissa are still all blissed out with each other after twelve years together.

Larissa shuffles over to the table and sits down while I sit the boys in their high-chairs.

"Aren't you going to be late?" I ask.

She shakes her head. "Trial starts at eleven."

"Huh." I start to feed the babies, but my mind wanders off, back to yesterday, to

Nat in her filthy clothes and how badly I wished I'd kissed her under the porch. "Hey, Larissa…can I ask you something?"

"Am I in trouble?"

"No." Avery gleefully spits banana all over the place. "But I might be. Well, not 'trouble,' exactly."

"Let me try to wake up a little then." She sits up and rubs her face. "Sounds serious."

"It's about Nat." Felix mucks his hands in the goo on his highchair.

"Uh-huh." Larissa nods. "Talk to me."

"Well, yesterday she was here and there was this moment when I—" Felix smacks his lips and grins at me. Suddenly it all seems very unlikely, like my imagination was making up life where there was just boredom. "Never mind."

Larissa shakes her head. "Talk to me, Hope."

"It's just that—" Geez, I wish I didn't blush so easily.

"Wait a minute, I know where this is going…" Larissa sets her coffee down. "She made a pass at you, didn't she?"

"So she is?" I asked.

"Is what?"

"Gay?"

"Was there any doubt?" Larissa laughs. She raps my head. "Is your gaydar out of whack, hon?"

"Do I have a gaydar?"

"Doesn't everybody?" says Larissa.

I spoon some more bananas at the boys. "What does yours say about me?"

Larissa gets up for more coffee. "It says you're young."

"What's that supposed to mean?"

"It means whatever you want it to mean." She leans against the counter. "What do you want it to mean?"

"I don't know." I shrug.

"What happened yesterday?"

I tell her. "So? Do you think I'm crazy?"

"Not at all." Larissa shakes her head. "She wants you."

"Does that make me gay?"

"Someone coming on to you doesn't make you gay," Larissa laughs. "It's how you react that matters."

"Oh." I give up on the bananas and get a cloth to wipe the highchair trays.

"Oh? That's it? You're not going to tell me how you reacted?"

"I'm not sure." I wipe the highchairs, and then I get a facecloth and wipe the boys' faces and hands and set them on the rug with their toys, and all the while Larissa stares at me.

"What?" I say.

"It's okay," Larissa says. "You don't have to tell me. It's rude of me to ask. I'm sorry."

"Well, I think that maybe I wanted to kiss her. Maybe. I think."

"Wow." Larissa's eyes widen. "Is that a new thing for you? Girls, I mean?"

I nod, and then, all of a sudden, the giddiness I'd woken up with evaporates and terror sets in. What will Joy say? And everyone at the farm? And Nat? What if I'm way off and I'm really as straight as it gets and am just suffering from a fleeting moment of questioning because of my lesbian environs, and now I've laid my soul bare when I didn't need to? I should've kept my mouth shut, at least until

I'd kissed her. At least until I knew for sure. I feel my eyes well up. I am just one big human mood swing and I want off.

"Oh, Hope." Larissa hugs me as the tears let loose. "This is a big deal for you, huh?"

"I don't know," I say, gulping between sobs. "It's just weird, that's all."

"I came out in college," Larissa says. "Her name was Monica—"

"But I'm not coming out!" I cry even harder. "I don't know what's going on! That's the problem, don't you understand?"

"You do whatever you need to." Larissa's voice softens. "No one's going to jump to conclusions. Yourself included, okay?"

"Don't tell anyone, okay?"

Larissa nods.

"Even Maira, okay?"

"Okay." Larissa sits herself with the boys on the rug. "How about you go take a shower or a walk or something before I go?"

I nod. "Thanks, Larissa."

Larissa shrugs. "Not sure that I helped, but you're welcome."

Chapter Eight

I take Daisy for a walk in the park, which doesn't clear my mind much because I keep thinking I see Nat and Clocker in the distance, and I'm not even sure if I want to run into her or never see her again so long as I live. When I get back, Larissa leaves for her trial, and I pack the twins into the double stroller and go wandering the neighborhood, trying to distract myself with the bustle of Brooklyn. It doesn't work.

I end up just up a block from the bike shop where Nat works. I try to tell myself it isn't on purpose, but the fact is that I want to see her. Need to, actually. I need to know if I still want to kiss her, because if I don't, then I don't have anything to worry about. Back to business as usual, right? Maybe Bruce has some younger friends he could set me up with. Actually, come to think of it, that could be a very good idea. A tidy little summer fling in New York with some studly actor wannabe? I can think of worse things…and besides, this whole kissing girls thing is probably just a phase.

That'd be just like me. I've always been impressionable. Like when the Buddhist Woofers came to the farm and I wanted to be a Buddhist. And when the fire spinners came and I wanted to go on tour with them, just like that. And then there was my vegan phase and my Wicca phase and my militant anti-fur phase. So maybe this is just a case of me being some kind of unoriginal queer wannabe? How pathetic that I don't even know myself well enough to know if I like boys or girls. Or both?

One of the bike mechanics is sitting outside smoking. I'm a bundle of nerves, so I hustle right past and all the way down to the end of the block, where I shake my head in wonder. Why hadn't I gone in?

I look back. Nat has joined the mechanic on the bench. She's sitting in the shade, but I can tell it's her, and after just that one glance I also know something else. I am no queer wannabe. This is no phase. This is for real. Real, like breathing. Real, like lightning sheets in summer storms. Real, like my pounding heart and racing thoughts. *Real*. Uh-oh.

I'm in big trouble. Not only do I still want to kiss her, but I *have* to kiss her. And I know it for sure from all the way at the end of the block. I don't think she's seen me. I should take off before she does so I don't do anything I might regret. But I'm stuck, transfixed, staring at her as she stands and moves into the sun, still talking to the mechanic. They both squat to check out a bike. Seconds later, she stands to grab a passing girl in a hug. They laugh, and she lifts the cute girl with blue hair right off her feet.

Uh-oh.

I'm in bigger trouble than I thought. I'm jealous! I yank the stroller around and turn the corner. I sit on a bench outside a store and take a deep, steadying breath. Get a grip, Hope.

I check on the babies. They're both still sleeping. Imagine being so little and fresh and new to the world…right now their lives are perfect and unblemished. Just you wait, little guys. My life, on the other hand…I put my head in my hands and give it all a great big think.

Okay, so I obviously have a crush on Nat. I might be new to the whole girl thing, but I'm not new to how being crushed out feels. This is a crush of the highest order. It's about way more than a kiss now.

Suddenly I'm in somebody's shadow. Sigh. I don't have to look up to know it's Nat.

"Hey," she says.

I keep my head in my hands. "Hi?"

"You went right past and you didn't come in."

"So you followed me?"

She doesn't say anything, so I look up. There she is, flashing that smile again. "That's right."

"Okay."

"Okay, what?"

I shrug and replace my head in my hands.

"Hey, Hope." She taps my shoulder.

I don't look up. "Yeah?"

"Something the matter?"

I laugh. I guess I have to look up now, before she starts to think that I'm some kind of social retard. "It's nothing. Never mind."

"It's something."

"I think I'm just homesick, that's all," I say.

She sits beside me on the bench, very close, considering there's the whole bench to be had.

"Miss your friends?"

I shake my head. "Not as much as I miss my parents."

"Wow. That's unusual," she laughs.

"We're really close." Touchy subject. I can feel the tears already. "They're in Thailand, building a school, so it's not like I can just pick up the phone and call them and tell them—" Time to shut up, Hope.

Nat lifts her arm in that classic "gonna-drape-it-across-your-shoulders" move, but instead she clasps her hands together and sets them in her lap. "Ice cream?"

"Now?"

"I think you are in desperate need of some Uncle Louie G's Peanut Butter Thrill."

"I don't like Peanut Butter Thrill."

"Okay." She stands and stretches. "So, what do you like?"

Sigh. Why does everything she says seem like a come-on?

"Chocolate Commotion." Thank the Universe that we are sitting in the shade and my out-of-control blushing isn't so obvious.

"Correction, then." She takes my hand and pulls me up. "I think you are in desperate need of some of Uncle Louie G's Chocolate Commotion. Come on." She lets go of my hand. "My treat."

I clutch the stroller, afraid that if I don't hold onto something with both hands I'll throw myself at her and chuck her to the ground and try out that kiss right here in the middle of the sidewalk, or, at the very least, grab her hand back and cling to it for dear life. Orion used to tease me that I was a pouncer. Maybe he was right.

Nat shoves her hands into her pockets and I push the stroller, and together we walk to Uncle Louie G's in near silence, the dogs trailing behind us, collecting their pee-mail. I really, truly, madly want to know what she's thinking, and if that wasn't such a murdered line, I might ask. She buys the ice cream, and we sit at one of the tables to eat it.

"How can you just leave work any time you want?" I ask, proud of myself for finding a safe topic.

"I'm the boss," she says.

"What?"

"I own the shop."

"Wow, that's cool."

"You know how you're close to your parents?" Nat says.

I nod, trying to keep up with my melting ice cream.

"Well I'm not."

"Oh. Sorry."

"They're big into God." Nat shrugs. "And not so big into me being me."

"My parents are the kind who love for their kids to be a little freaky. They think it reflects positively on their parenting. They're hippies. "

"Yeah, Maira told me the other day when she brought in the bike trailer for the babies. I think she's jealous." Nat gives her waffle cone to Clocker. "Anyway, my parents bought me the shop, basically to keep me out of their hair. They've got a chain of used car lots in Iowa. They didn't exactly want me in the family business."

"How old are you?" I ask.

"Nineteen."

"That's not so bad," I blurt.

"What do you mean?"

I mean the age gap is far better than the one with Orion, but I'm not about to tell her that. "The setup with your parents."

"You know I'm queer, right?"

"Yeah, Larissa told me." A rush of heat

floods my cheeks and belly. I focus on what's left of my ice cream.

Nat laughs. "Probably warned you is my guess."

I gulp, hoping the knot in my stomach will ease. My heart races. I'm really just a colossal mess, like the toddler at the next table who's covered in strawberry ice cream from head to toe. "What makes you say that?"

"You're my type. And they both know it."

"Wow." My head finds its way back into my hands again.

"Oh. Shit." Nat touches me, but then pulls away. "Sorry. I didn't mean...well, I did mean, but not if you aren't—or don't— "

But I do! I do! I feel a pounce coming on. Will I? Really? Right here outside Uncle Louie G's?

"Are you okay?"

I force myself to look at her. I am way past just wanting to kiss her. The word "ravage" comes to mind. "I'm your type? Really?"

"Cute, smart, funny." Nat grins. "Want me to go on?"

She has her hands placed firmly on her thighs, as if she's holding herself down. I lift one of her hands in mine. I cannot believe I'm making a move on her, but at the same time, how can I not? I'm about to take off into the stratosphere without her, so I have to hold on or I'll leave her behind. She stares at her hand in mine. We both stand up, as if we're going to bolt in opposite directions, and our holding hands is the only thing stopping us.

"I like you, Hope." She stares at our hands. "You know that, right?"

"Not until right this minute." I think this means I wasn't making any of it up. I do have a gaydar! "Wow. That's really cool."

"Really?"

"I think so, but I'm kind of new to this."

"Which part?"

"The girl parts." I drop her hand. "I cannot believe I just said that."

She starts laughing, and then we both crack up.

When we're down to giggles, she takes my hand back. "Now?"

"Now what?"

"You know what."

And so I kiss her, just a little one on the cheek, and then I linger my lips there and move them toward hers. "This?" I whisper.

"Exactly this." She holds the back of my neck and pulls me to her and kisses me back, and within seconds she has officially surpassed all eleven boys on my kissed list and moved right into first place. She slides the hand at my neck down my back and into the pocket of my shorts. She takes my other hand with her free one, and then she pulls away.

"I'm going to ask you out and you're not going to say no, are you?" She laughs. "I don't even have to ask, because that kiss…*that* was my answer. Wow."

The teenage guys working at Uncle Louie G's wolf whistle at us.

"Yeah, baby!" The taller one rubs his hands together. "Do it again!"

"Shut up, Julio!" Nat flashes him the finger and then touches my cheek. "And I hope you don't have a problem with being out, because this is as out as it gets, girl."

"C'mon. Why you get more action than us, huh?" Julio hollers. "What you got I don't?"

"You'd like to know, man." Nat laughs again and then squeezes my hand. "Right outside Louie G's! You are something else!"

"I have to sit for a second." I feel like my life just leapt off its course and is careening toward a brand-new me. It's all more than a little overwhelming.

"Are you okay?"

"Definitely." I nod. "Better than okay, just a little shaky."

"I'm your first girl?"

I nod again.

"Ever?"

"First girl. Ever."

"Well, hey, welcome to the club."

"But I wanna be in your club!" Julio hollers. "I want to be a lesbo too!"

"I'll see what I can do, Julio." Nat pulls me up. "Come on, let's get out of here."

Chapter Nine

Maira and Larissa have both heard about Nat and me by the time they get home from work.

"Julie from the food co-op saw you two," Maira says as she lifts Avery into her arms.

"And she phoned Maira," Larissa helps herself to Felix and coos at him in a singsong voice, "and then Mommy phoned Mama and pretty soon all the dykes in Brooklyn will know how we corrupted that poor young slip of a thing from out west. Isn't that right?" Felix grabs at her nose and giggles.

"So?" Maira dances Avery around the kitchen. "Tell us everything. And no, Larissa didn't tell me anything I didn't already know."

I'd been chopping carrots when they walked in. I look at the knife and at the carrots and think back over the afternoon. It is amazing and dreamy and hot and scary and not something I want to share with them at all. Besides, I'm supposed to be looking after the boys, not making out with some girl. But she isn't just "some girl." She is far more than that.

"I don't know what to say." An enormous grin slides across my face.

"Oh! Look at the look on her!" Larissa sticks Felix in my face. "Look at her, Felix!"

Felix babbles happily at me, trying to grab my nose too.

"Should we throw you a coming out party?" Maira says.

I ignore the carrots. This is all so weird, and cutting carrots is just so normal, and somehow the two do not go together. I plunk myself down at the table.

"I can honestly tell you that I don't know anything about anything at all," I say.

Larissa and Maira share another one of their looks.

"Too much?" Maira says.

"Too fast?" Larissa says.

"And totally none of our business," Maira finishes. "Are we on the right track?"

"That's just it." I yank a flower from the arrangement on the table and start pulling it apart. "I don't know. It just seems like life is really hard if you're a person who's alive."

"This is true." Larissa offers me another flower to demolish. "But think of the alternative. That's no fun."

They leave me to myself and finish making supper while I annihilate the flower arrangement. After we eat, they take the babies out for a stroll and I wander the empty house, willing the phone to ring. She said she'd call. I carry the portable phone with me as I meander restlessly from one room to another. Should I just call her?

I pull the piece of paper out of my pocket. She wrote her number in huge black digits, like it's yelling at me to call her. I start dialing, but of course, obedient to the cliché, I hang up before it rings.

Maira and Larissa come back, armed with movies and microwave popcorn, and we all settle in to watch some brain-dead action movie, which they'd picked especially for me.

"Doesn't use any gray matter," Maira says.

"So you can use all available gray matter for other matters," Larissa finishes.

The phone rings halfway through the movie, and because I'm still clutching it, I answer it before the first ring finishes.

"Hey," Nat says.

"Hey," I say.

And then we both get a serious case of the unstoppable giggles. Maira kicks me out of the room, so I dash upstairs, flop onto the bed, and we get ourselves under control.

"So, can I take you to Coney Island tomorrow?"

"Absolutely."

"Wait a second, let me twist your arm."

And then hours pass in a few fleeting seconds, or it's the other way around, or something, anyway. Time is huge and at the same time it is tiny. It's after midnight when we finally hang up, with plans to meet at the subway in the morning.

Chapter Ten

We hold hands on the train, all the way out to Coney Island, and it doesn't feel weird at all. Some people stare, and a Hassidic mother frowns and hustles her children to the other end of the car, but I don't care. We get off the train and buy iced coffees and peroshki at a Russian deli and then walk barefoot across the hot sand to the water's edge. It's a weekday, but the beach is still crowded, with so many colorful children and toys and towels and sun umbrellas that I imagine we look like a spill of beautiful jewels from above.

It's windy and hot and loud and feels like we're all teetering at the edge of the planet. Nat cartwheels along the beach and then does a series of backflips, supposedly for a pack of shirtless little boys who don't speak English at all, although I'm more impressed than anyone, I'm sure. The boys cheer her on, in Russian, I think, and then follow us along the board-walk to the freak show. Nat gives them each a quarter, and they run off toward the arcade.

"Want to go in?"

"I'm not old enough."

Nat winks. "I can hook us up."

She knows the girl who swallows swords, so I soon find myself in a dim little theater with wooden bleachers and a sad, rickety stage. The lights go down. Nat kisses me and takes my hand.

"I've never brought a girl to the freak show before," she whispers.

"So what should I think?"

She kisses me again as the curtain rises. "You're pretty special, that's what I think."

We watch her friend swallow swords. There are flame eaters and knife throwers and a man who hangs weights from fresh piercings, and another man who can contort himself through a tennis racket with the strings removed, and a woman who lies on a bed of nails with the sword swallower standing on her belly. Life is like that, really—a stunning, painful stunt, yet magically endurable.

When we emerge into the hot, blue daylight, we make our way to the train and go home, tired and sunburnt and blissed out on each other.

Later, Nat comes with me to Joy's because my parents are supposed to call. Joy isn't home, although she'd promised Bruce would make us his famous spaghetti that I've heard so much about and never actually had. I told her about Nat, and she told me it was a phase that she'd gone through too—but she says that about everything, so who knows, really? I bet the only comment Joy will make when she meets Nat is about her dreads. Joy hates dreadlocks on white people.

Joy's cell phone is sitting on the table

beside a twenty-dollar bill and a note. I don't think I've ever seen her separated from her phone, but judging by the note, which suggests I order pizza with the twenty, I'd say she's feeling a little guilty about the prank she pulled on me. We order pizza and then wait for the call.

"What are you going to tell them?" Nat says. We're spooned on the chaise lounge in the dark, the sound of the summer evening street slipping in the open window.

"I don't know." And I don't, right up until the phone actually rings. I've been so looking forward to talking to my parents, but I'm suddenly terrified of the little silver thing, shimmying its way across the table as it plays some brain-dead club-track ring tone.

I answer it. "Mom?"

"What, you think your old man can't work a satellite phone?"

"Daddy!"

"Daddy?" The connection crackles and pops. "Is something the matter?"

"No, no, no. Everything's fine." And it is, I suddenly realize. It really, truly, honestly is.

"Everything is great! I met someone really spectacular."

"Oh? Let me tell your mother." I hear them talk, muffled, and then he's back. "Your mother has her ear mashed up to the phone."

"Hi, honey!" she says, her voice a little tiny scratch in the static. "We love you!"

Dad's voice is much clearer. "What am I thinking right now?" he asks.

"Okay, wait." I close my eyes and put my fingers to my temples. "Okay, I'm ready."

"I'm sending it to you," Dad says.

And I get the clearest picture of the two of them, on a beach, tanned and grinning, waving at me. I open my eyes and describe it to him.

"That's right!" my mom says, although I can barely hear her.

"Your turn, kiddo."

"Okay, wait." I send him a picture of me and Nat on the beach. She's doing the back-flips for the little boys, and the wind is fierce, and I'm holding my hair out of my face.

"I got it loud and clear. You're doing

great," Dad says. "That's what I got. That you're having the time of your life."

"You're right, Dad." This one isn't in the details, but he nailed it nonetheless.

"So who is he?"

My heart skips, but just a little. "Her name is Nat." I glance over at her. She has her hands behind her head and is watching me, grinning. "And she's amazing."

"Well, how about that?" There's a short symphony of static, and then the connection is so clear I can hear my dad breathing. "You're happy?"

"More than ever before."

"Well," he says, "then I am thrilled for you."

"Me too, sweetheart," my mom adds, her voice almost as clear as Dad's.

I join Nat on the couch. She sits behind me and puts her arms around me while I tell them all about Nat. Then I put the cell on speaker-phone and we listen, heads together, as my parents describe the Larchberry Thailand Project and how my dad managed to fry his GPS watch and the laptop within the first week, and how, when they get back, they want to have a proper wedding, with a gown and a tux and a caterer and vows and rings.

"And you'll have to invite your Nat," Mom says, taking the phone from Dad. Nat grins and gives me the thumbs-up.

I'm in! she mouths.

Dad takes the phone back. "She's not one of those I-hate-vegetarians New Yorkers like Joy has turned into, is she?"

"No I'm not, sir," Nat pipes in. "Long live tofu!"

"Is that her?" Dad says.

"Yeah," I say. "She's been listening in."

"Well give the phone to her for a minute."

"Okay, Dad." I'm not going to waste precious time explaining to a technophobe that cell phones have speaker options. "Here she is."

"Hello, sir," Nat says.

"Call me Marv, none of that sir or ma'am mumbo jumbo," Dad says. I stifle a laugh. "Now, I'm going to tell you one thing and ask you one thing."

"Yes, sir?" Nat shakes her head. "I mean, Marv."

"Our Hope is more precious to us than anything, and she deserves to be loved by a brilliant, true heart and nothing less. Understand?"

I get shivers, hearing him talk to Nat like this. Love? True hearts? He's never done this before. Maybe their wedding plans have sent him into a mushy tailspin?

"I couldn't agree more," Nat grins, "Marv."

"And all I ask is that you be true to each other and to yourselves."

"I think that's how we ended up…"

"Ended up what?" I whisper.

Nat kisses me on the cheek and then speaks toward the phone. "I think that's how we ended up girlfriends, sir."

"Good to hear," Dad says. "But please, call me Marv."